I Missed Woodstock

Bengt O Björklund

Published by Human Error Publishing
Paul Richmond
www.humanerrorpublishing.com
paul@humanerrorpublishing.com

Copyright © 2020
by
Human Error Publishing & Bengt O Björklund
All Rights Reserved

ISBN: 978-0-9991985-4-4
Photos by: Bengt O Björklund

Cover by Human Error Publishing
&
Bengt O Björklund

Translated by Bengt O Björklund

Edited by Debbie Tosun Kilday
&
Human Error Publishing

Table of Content

Intro   6

Where I came from   8

Visible   32

My Universities   68

The Return   106

New Goals   116

Postlude   118

Intro

When I left Sweden in the early fall of 1968 the world was full of possibilities. You could travel with no problem from Europe to India overland.

The influence India had on the Beat and the Hippie generations was immense indeed. We all wanted the spiritual hereness to expand each living day, we loved to walk around in light Indian garments, to put the same stuff in our chillums that the Sadhus did. We meditated and chanted. We read the old scriptures.

The music scene was marvellous. New intricate ways to make and perform music saw the light of every day and there was a promise that united us all, dreaming of a more fantastic and loving world.

Together with Alice I left Sweden in the early fall of 1968, hitchhiking through Europe, aiming for India. At that time Persia, Afghanistan and Pakistan were free of extremism and easy to travel through. There were many stories of the hospitality of the people in these countries, not forgetting Kathmandu and Nepal.

The Magic Bus went from Amsterdam to India, loaded with expectant young adults, hoping to find what they were looking for.

This is what happened on the European side during the late sixties. In the US the hippie culture turned into a green cheeky dragon in many parts of the country. So many fantastic bands came from hot spots in California, Illinois, New York and many more, not to forget the Canadian scene.

The world was a beating heart and we were all a part of that rhythm.

One night in a hotel room in Istanbul, around Christmas 1968, I lost all that, heading into emptiness. Heavily psychotic due to a heavy drug mixture overdose I was arrested a week later.

This is the story of possibilities in places you never dreamt of. It's the story of a will to survive and make a difference, in the end. It's a long, still ongoing, story about all of us. What is important? What is it that makes a person willing to supersede his own limitations and dare his circumstances to listen?

Finally.

Who I am today is a direct result of all my experiences.
I am an artist,
a poet
and a percussionist.
I still breathe the air
of a greatness
we once roamed.

Where I came from

In early 1943 she left on a kicksled
from her parents' home in Lugnvik
to go to her sister, in the small town of Multrå.
She was only sixteen years old,
and she would become my mother.

The journey continued –
first to a small shop in Sollefteå town,
where she worked for a few months,
then onwards to her sister Ingrid,
in the city of Västerås.

My mother was the youngest
of seven children.

Finally, she ended up in Stockholm in 1946,
where she met Olle
at the large LM Ericsson plant,
the man who would be my dad.

I was born at Sabbatsberg hospital
in mid-August 1949.
This I do not remember, of course,
nor my first year
after we moved into
the apartment on Arkövägen in Kärrtorp.

Our time in the suburb of Årsta
where my little sister Berit was born,
I do not remember either.

In 1955 my parents moved
into an apartment
on Majeldsvägen in Midsommarkransen,
another suburb south of Stockholm.
There my first
and oldest memories
still reside
although the street
has since been renamed

and is now called Tellusborgsvägen.
Little did I know
that mother was already
tiring of father.

***

We children were given lots of space,
our play areas expanded
in all directions every day.
Sometimes we played by the cliffs
behind the Brännkyrka high school,
climbing down dangerous precipices.

Today, only a few meters are left
of those dangerous cliffs,
leading down to the droning traffic
on the Essingeleden highway.

Other times we were
far down on the vast fields of Årsta
climbing huge coke stockpiles
left behind since the war.

***

One year I was in Ångermanland,
in the north of Sweden,
visiting my old grandfather
still living in Lugnvik.

On a visit to Aunt Eira
a cheeky Multrå mountain
seduced me with spectacular views,
and steep cliffs.

The road wound up through the forest,
abounding with spruce, pine,
mossy stones and ferns
breathing in the shadows.

At the top there was a small pavilion.
The rocks on the steep side called me.

On my way down the steep side,
I had to let go of one ledge
to fall to the next
in a sudden delirious rush.

Then it ended.
I could only continue
if I jumped across a wide crack
onto a new ledge.

I took a deep breath.
In that moment
I felt for the first time
my own mortality,
and an uncertainty
if there were more days to come,
in a sudden flash.

I grabbed hold of a shrub
and managed
to make my way back
to an anxiously awaiting
little sister
at the empty pavilion.

***

I started first grade at a school
on the other side of a busy main road,
in some makeshift barracks
at the back of the school.

We were only allowed
into the main building to have lunch.

***

It was not so long ago,
Holger, a friend, seven like me,
living in an apartment next to ours,
ran out onto the busy main road
instead of taking the detour
through the tunnel
on the way to school.

His weeping parents
unwittingly gave me the feeling
it must be my fault.
That feeling is still with me.

And yet here I am
still alive with Holger but
a memory amongst many.

Suddenly everything
can be over
before it really starts.

***

The new woman that
lived next door to my uncle
planted her intention in my father.
She was ostracized from her own family.

She seduced my father
causing what seemed inevitable,
convincing him to give up his present
and his past.
She said he must stop resisting.

In exchange,
he got two spoiled daughters
and later, a new son,
that I never met
until much later.
She made new demands,

no contact
with the past,
or the children left behind.
Focus on her girls was an ultimatum.

***

My mother stood on the balcony
calling to us kids
playing in the green area
between the trees
and the tenement houses,
a summer in the mid-fifties:

"You will get a dollar
if you find my ring!"
We searched frantically
to no avail.

She believed the ring
had been on the carpet
she just shook
from the first-floor balcony.

Many years later my little sister
told me she dropped it in the toilet,
got scared and flushed it
into oblivion.
She was only four at the time.

The ring was not a wedding ring,
but soon after that
the marriage was over.

***

Importance resided in shadows
where the meaning of words
densified in an ominous way.

I knew I was about
to lose something familiar,
but did not know what.

From the kitchen,
I heard angry voices.

Outside the window,
the sound of tires,
a car passed by
on an autumn-wet street.

This was my first
real night
alive
and a bit outside it all.
The starting point of my voyage.

***

We moved to the suburb of Blackeberg,
mother, Berit and I.
Amongst all the belongings
that came with us
to the new apartment
there was no trace of my father.

I continued first grade
in a new school
in the middle of the semester of 1957.
I had to go alone
with longing and confusion.

I was shy and lost, and
I placed myself at the back of the classroom
with thirty other children.
We started at eight
and ended at four.
Saturdays we stopped at one.

***

When the bell rang
hopscotch in chalk,
oblique squares
hastily drawn on the tarmac,
were hastily abandoned
and the queue by the skip rope
slowly dissipated.

Proud owners of new moviestar cards
- you got them
with your chewing gum -
looked tenderly at their new acquisitions,
a Doris Day for a Lana Turner,
a John Wayne for a Roy Rogers.

When I was sick
I played with Victorian scraps,
cutouts of Indians and cowboys,
fighting in the rolling landscape in the bed
with mountains and prairies.

The scraps came in sheets,
riding cowboys
and bare back Indians.

It was the Indians
that usually won.

***

I do not remember much
of how we celebrated our Christmases,
but I do remember
that our Christmas tree
had Nordic flags on strings,
a spire of glass
and plaited paper hearts.

Often, I listened to Uncle Sven
and the Secret Club, glued to the radio.
I was a member,
and I followed Froggy Ball, Grassy Hopper
and Tin-Nikolas of course.

An episode of a submarine
sailing up a small river made a special
and magical impression.
I dreamt of traveling secretly in dark waters.

**

My father left a gramophone behind
that he had built himself.
The pin was made of bronze
and it was 78's that were played.

One day I found a 78 record
with the words
"thunder and snuff and furry sluts"
in the lyrics
and carried it down to my friend Kennet
who lived downstairs.

We listened and laughed until we choked.
When I heard my mother
on her way home
I hurried upstairs,
stumbled and dropped the record.
It broke into a thousand pieces.
Not even numerous excuses
could save me from a whipping.
I hid under the bed.

**

We had a special game in school.
We hyperventilated,

then squeezed someone hard over the chest.
I was the best at fainting.

One time I hit my head so hard
on the school yard asphalt
I got a concussion.

Me and Halvar
were always bullied.
We did not have so much
in common,
but at least we were bullied together.

***

Tidings came
late at night.
I was asleep. Dreaming.

I had to go to heaven
to be beheaded by an angel.

Other nights
the presence of witches
filled the woods
with a premonition
of something horrible,
terrifying, and paralyzing.
I now knew of my mortality.

***

Pine bark and pinecones,
moss and lava,
sticks and small rocks,
everything turned
into a farmer's landscape
on a south-facing mountain slope
where the snow first melted
in the early days of spring 1957.

The snow-covered wetlands
between the forest and the mountain
now embrace the dead.

***

All days had their origin
in a birth,
in a gentle rain over a forest
that talked to me so many times.
I am still there.
I am still here.

Tracks and trails
rarely trodden by others
left imprints on my green eyes.

Singing hares allured me,
smelling of wet herbs
and spicy marshes.

***

The coot was stuck,
surprised
by the sudden ice chill of night.
It was stuck in the ice
of the frozen lake Mälaren water.

Once home I filled our tub with water.
It stayed there for a few days,
but died anyway,
surrounded by breadcrumbs.
It was a nice funeral.

A shoe box, dressed in velvet,
went down the garbage chute.
A goodbye in tears.

***

Often, we broke into a huge house
clad in corrugated iron.
We called it the Haunted House.
At night we crawled on a plank
in through a broken window.

It was once a storage house
for the water mill next door.

***

I would often rest on a large willow branch
leaning out over the lake Mälaren
fishing without a float
waiting for anything to bite.

The hook was covered
with wet bread,
lovingly kneaded with saliva
to stick.

I did not see much
of what happened
beneath the water surface,
the pull of the line
was my cue.

I caught bream and perch.
Mom cooked them.
Bream had so many bones.

***

The scent of lake Mälaren
gave a unique touch
to my encounter with free water.
The scent of reeds and wet sand
followed me like a belonging
in balmy summer nights.
My wet swimwear

carried that poignant scent.
It was the same fragrance that lingered
on the wet skin of the young girls
my longing inhaled.
A longing great and boundless
as I watched them undress
through the peep-hole
behind their beach dressing room.

***

Going to school
didn't really work out.
I often felt lost where I sat
at the back of the classroom.

I was often teased for my shyness.
It was just Ulf, living in the apartment
below me, that occasionally
was on my side.
But he moved away one day with his mother
shortly after his father,
a military officer,
crashed in a banana helicopter.

I remember seeing the wreck
on the front page of the dailies.

***

In 1958, I got a new baby sister.
She was very cute
and named Susanne.

Her father was a sailor.
He had brought
two big earthenware pots with him
from the Canary Islands,
ending up in the window
of the living room.

Many years later,
they would be severly discolored
when I used them as hookahs.

***

I often cut class
and spent my time
in the woods around Blackeberg,
Southern Ängby and Grimsta.

In the white winter magic
that hung heavily
from pine and spruce,
I found peace and silence.
Sometimes I made fires
between stones in the snow
toasting slices of white bread.

I could read fox and bird tracks,
deer and badgers
that left their calligraphic impressions
across the vast expanse of snow
belonged to me.
I was happy there.

***

The snow covered the trees
with a frozen sea
of white, glistening waves.
The magic of my ubiquitous solitude
gave the landscape
a very strong belonging.

I learned a lot about animals
and often saw them.
A white lonely grandeur prevailed
around my blue wooden skis,
a quiet, white stillness.

***

I lived with my two sisters
in the same small bedroom.
It faced a very big yard
with tall pine trees.

I slept in the top bunk
above Berit,
Sussie slept in a bed by the window.
I had a small string bookshelf
above my head.

The shelves were filled
with books by Enid Blyton
and books on zoology and botany.

Mom slept in the kitchen.
The living room was spotless.
That's how we lived
until the day
I did not come home.

***

One summer we strung a metal wire
over the large yard.
I climbed the bare trunks
of the tall pines
to connect the wire to the branches.
At both ends there was a tin can.
We could make out pretty well
what the other one was saying.

***

We had a homemade trapeze
tied to a pine branch.
The tree grew on the embankment
of a subway bridge.

22

When I threw myself
out from the top,
I flew high above the ground
before landing
on the other side of the tree trunk.

One day Halvar lost his grip
and fell. He broke his arm
and I told him he was clumsy.

The next day the rope broke
when I swung out.
Then we were two dunces
with plastered arms in the class.

***

Me and Kennet competed one day
with our folded paper swallows.
Wondering which one would fly the farthest?

From the 12th floor entry
to a roof space
where carpets were beaten
we made it to the edge
of the flat roof
of this baby blue high-rise building.
We laid on our stomachs,
twelve floors up.

It took forever
before the paper swallows landed.
Sometimes the wind caught them
and they soared high into the sky
before slowly returning to earth.
I do not remember
who won.

***

In a slow-moving
and unspoken lament
my father faded away
and uncertainty
affected me
as something inexplicable
vulnerable and naked.

Emptiness became a negation,
a denial
of what once was,
a subdued shadow
that scared me.

***

I never learned to wolf-whistle
like the other kids.
The fingers never ended up
where they were supposed to
in my mouth,
or had it something to do with my tongue?

The small plastic guitars
came in various colors
and with conviction
we pinned them on our jackets.
Either you had Elvis Presley
or you had Tommy Steele
pinned to your lapel.
I was all in for Tommy.

***

When I was in fourth grade
at the Blackeberg school
we made pipes from acorns,
picked on the meadow
below the Blackeberg hospital.
we filled the pipes with shavings

24

from the pencil sharpener.
It tasted awful
but it felt
like a step on the way.

***

I was ashamed of my eczema
when it was time for gymnastics.
My socks were often stuck
in clotted blood
and I could not get them off.
It worked better
when it was time for swimming lessons
in the small pool next door.
The water from the shower
loosened the stubborn socks.

The times I did do
gymnastics I liked the
game
when you are not
allowed
to touch the floor at
all.
No one could climb up
a rope faster than I.

***

Every autumn I had to cut my hair,
all of it...
One fall semester
I was called The Egg in my class.
I was so embarrassed.

***

Each summer,
I was a "summer child".

I had to go away to a new family
somewhere in Sweden

So many summers spent
with strangers up and down
the country, paid for
by the city of Stockholm.

Every year the same tears
at the Central Station:
I do not want to!

One summer
I was on the island of Öland.
At the same time
my baby sister was there
with a different family.
I managed to make it
on foot
all the way
to where she was.

I remember the joy I felt
walking that dusty road
with her little hand in mine.

In the county of Östergötland
I learned to run naked
across meadows and pastures
amongst surprised cows.

I was taught to swim in Lake Boren,
came to hate Corn Flakes
and caught crayfish
in a small lake a few kilometers
into the thick forest.
Between the towns
of Motala and Borensberg
I learned to ride a bike
on a dirt road with ditches full of nettles.

It stung every time
I fell off the bike.
In Skåne, I ran across the dunes
towards the chalk blond Ylva,
a lovely snowstorm on the way to the sea,
a cherry tree caught by the wind.

Another summer
I was on the island of Gotland
harvesting cucumbers on a farm.
I weeded large fields all day long
and learned to drive a tractor.

There I met Linda, nine years old,
I was twelve and in love.
Fall on me here, she said firmly,
pointing to a specific place
high up in the hayloft.

Then there was Eve, fifteen,
peeing in the middle of the road.
without blushing.

***

We children used to ride
our bikes
to a villa area of Norra Ängby,
come summer come winter,
just to look at the Creation.
When it was summer,
we snuck into his garden
filching the fruit we could reach.

Sometimes he came out
dressed only in a bath robe,
his anger shining bright
in his dark hair.

His eyes shattrered
like broken northern waters,
surged, angry,
spoke of distance and a pain
we did not understand.
What he called himself
I do not know,
but what he was waiting for was obvious.
The boat he had built on his roof
stood there all throughout my childhood years
waiting for the flood.

***

One day in December, my father
took me and my sister Berit
to a Christmas party
at the Stockholm tram
and bus main depot.

There was something magical
about this moment,
this return.

Two slightly older girls
showed up and said, offended,
that "this is our father,
not at all yours"
and they started an argument.
I felt sad.

***

A few men came and went
in my mother's life.
The sailor I do not remember,
The bricklayer let me be the handyman
one summer building a house in Skuru
on top of a hill by the sea.

The electrician had an office
on Holländargatan street,
smack in the middle
of downtown Stockholm.
They each made a sudden entrance
and after a while a silent exit.

***

One early summer day
I was admitted
to the Sankt Göran Hospital
for an allergy check up.
I ended up in a small room
on the ground floor.
I could climb out of the window.

I spent day after day
walking
the hospital grounds.

Down the slopes,
where they grew vegetables
above the Shell gas station,
I got to know Sven,
who was usually there
taking care of the greens.

Sven, or as he was called, Chicago,
was the man who ran
the stainless-steel food carts
in long shiny trains
billowing through kilometer-long
culverts under the hospital.

Electronic eyes opened doors for the train
and I hid by those doors,
waiting for the train to come.
I jumped the last car
and clung on to it

for the sheer joy of it,
station to station,
from surgery to palliative care.

One day, I discovered that
the big payphone
outside my ground floor ward
just needed a gentle nudge
to erupt into a handful of small coins.
Cookies and lemonade
were back on the menu.

Weeks later,
after all the dot tests on my back
had been carefully studied
there was a diagnosis:
You are allergic to daisies...

***

I pressed flowers,
collected beetles and butterflies.
I immersed myself
with lizards and frogs.

One early summer,
I studied birds with my binoculars
by the Råcksta marshland,
also called The Swamp.
By the shore I found a waterlogged raft.

Once out on the rotten water,
I aimed for the heavy clumps of reed,
thick with secrets and magical bird worlds.
Then the raft was stuck.
I could only stand on one side,
otherwise it would tip over.

It was stuck in old rubble
just below the dark forbidden surface.

I was going nowhere.
After an eternity,
I could see more and more people
gathering on the soft slopes
facing the water.
Then the fire brigade turned up
with jaunty uniforms
and a shiny aluminum boat.
The slopes were now full of people
smiling and applauding
the fire brigade.
I was so embarrassed.

***

I often rode my bike
out to the Bromma airport
to see the airplanes
take off and land.

When the first ever jet, a Caravelle landed
I was there.
The short runway
demanded a very special parachute.

Visible

When I started lower secondary class
at the Blackeberg high school,
all shyness suddenly vanished.
I sat in the front row.
On the very first day,
when we had history,
the class got the question:
What kind of ruler
reigns in England?
I raised my hand and answered:
The kind that smacks your fingers.

I was the clown of the class now
singled out for my bold antics;
no longer laughed at,
no longer bullied, ignored
and constantly on the run.

The tough guys
belonged to me now:
I was visible,
but I did not inhale
paint fumes, thinner
or glue.

***

We called our new teacher The Hairdo
because of his water combed hair
parted in the middle.
He got no respect,
the whole class made fun of him.

We screwed his ledger
between the panes of the window
facing the courtyard.

One day
he was ten minutes late.
We saw him approaching

and the whole class jumped
like falling water out the window,
onto the courtyard,
before he had walked down
the long empty corridor.

We used to put thumbtacks
underneath his seat cushion.

We were terrible.
I got an F
for bad conduct
and another F for not being neat

***

In the winter of 1963 Sweden got the silver medal
at the Ice Hockey World Championships
at the Ice Stadium in Stockholm.
Soviet won the gold
and the bronze went to Czechoslovakia.

I spent days outside
the hotel Malmen
on the Götgatan street.
I finally got almost all
the Czechoslovak team's
autographs.

I was very proud
of Jaroslav Jirik's scribble
in my little notebook.

***

In eighth grade,
we got a substitute teacher
who worked at Swedish Television.
She arranged for the whole class
to be in the audience

for many Drop-in recordings
hosted by Kersti Adams-Ray
and Klas Burling.

I particularly liked
the session with The Beatles
when Paul McCartney
asked the audience to clap their hands
and stamp their feet,
before they kicked off
into Twist and Shout.

That become a turning point.
The music echoed of something
that felt so familiar,
like something I'd waited for.

***

I bought a snare drum,
and a hi-hat
in a music store
by the Kronoberg Park
in central Stockholm.

Together with Krister and Göran
I started playing.
Our first song was
Under the boardwalk.

We rehearsed in my bedroom
where we recorded the music
on my Tandberg tape recorder.

***

The alluring city
had me looking for
still-valid subway tickets.

People threw them
into orange cast iron
wastebaskets
when they came out
of the station.

Later, when the first
monthly commuter card came,
we climbed over the fence
at the end of the platform.
We could not - would not - pay.

We ran up the wooden stairs
up the embankment,
climbed over the fence,
jumped the electric rail
and stepped onto the platform.

***

We would usually go to downtown Odenplan,
where we boarded the number seven
blue tram going to Skansen,
(a big park made on a hill
on the peninsula of Djurgården
with zoo and museums),
without paying, hiding in the crowd.

One time it was my father
that stood there
behind his small table
in the tram,
selling and checking tickets.
He did not see me.
The trick was to stay as far back
as possible
if you could not pay.

At one place in the fence
above some cliffs,

close to the last gate of Skansen
along the side were the tram went,
it was possible to squeeze in
between the thick metal bars.
The little money we had
was spent on ice cream,
but we were mainly
checking out the young chicks
with a new longing.

***

For two days I was tested
by a psychologist to find out
what my inherent abilities were.
I had to assemble jigsaw puzzles
and answer so many questions.

After two days the psychologic test
gave a clear answer:
obviously, the kid is to become
a car mechanic.

Thus I started my last, ninth, year
of public school.
One week at school,
The next at a mechanical workshop.

One day I dipped my hands in oil
and set them afire.
Flames bloomed on my fingers
to my classmates great amusement.
I put my hands in water
before I burned myself.

***

The autumn after
the ninth grade,
I started at the St. Erik's

vocational school,
down by the Klara Channel
in the center of Stockholm.

After a semester
trying to evolve into
car mechanic material,
any hope for that future
was definitely dashed.
I was not at all suited
they said.

A new trial as an construction carpenter
the following spring
brought the same result
with a wooden toolbox made so askew
and really, a general disinterest.

***

Stockholm City started to attract me
with its underground meeting places
and illegal handshakes.
No profession in the world,
I thought,
can outsmart a cheeky bum.

***

I switched from pinstripes
to American army surplus.
Impo at Gamla Brogatan street
was the only store that supplied
what we wanted.
We were Swedish Mods.

Our green US army jackets
were completely overwritten
with names like
The Who, The Stones, Friends,

Pretty Things, Animals, Manfred Mann,
The Small Faces
and John Mayall and the Bluesbreakers.

I let my hair grow even longer
and hung out on a large terrace
overlooking the Stockholm Concert hall,
dominating the big square of Hötorget.
We often sat on the stairs of the Concert Hall
drinking warm beer and smoking dope
and of course we were at Plattan,
the square outside the subway T-Central Station.

Lebanese costs fifty cents a gram,
Moroccan twenty-five and Afghan forty.

***

In the summer of 1965 I turned sixteen.
Some of us sat on the stairs
of the Stockholm Concert Hall
taking it softly with beer and dope,
basking in the sun,
when a greasy rocker
with a mean Alsatian
shouted abuse and insult at us.

We chased him down the Kungsgatan street.
Our numbers increased as we ran,
windows were smashed
the first Hötorg riot was a fact.

The next weekend people
gathered en masse
at the Hötorget square
crowding the overlooking terrace.

As if on cue the rush began.
Mounted police with sabers
lost big time.

The weekend revolts
gave birth to
a new collected alienation:
the Mods generation,
making a stand
against a bourgeois adulthood,
war and political prophets.

***

Winter we usually spent
inside the Stockholm C subway station
if the police
didn't tell us to "circulate"
a police order in fashion.

Sometimes we would hang
at the 37th, a youth center
on the Drottninggatan street.
Later the 4th came,
another youth place
on the Gamla brogatan street.

I often met Stoffe and Kenta.
They belonged to
a different group of teenagers
living on the outskirts of society
unnoticed by most.

Stoffe came from Vällingby,
two stations away
from where I grew up.
I often met him on the subway
going into town.

We were probably a little jealous of them
with a film crew following them all day,
but concluded that they probably
were a bit to pleased with themselves.

***

Stig, my mother's man at the time,
had his own electric shop in the city.
He gave me a job
as a flatbed moped delivery boy.
One day I was down in Kungsan,
a landmark park in Stockholm,
to score some dope.
When I got back
the moped was stolen.

There was hell to catch.

***

I ended up being sent
to a Christian boarding school in the woods
outside the small city of Järna.
The idea was probably
a hope that I would atone
after recent contacts
with the justice system
and child welfare committees.

Or was I perhaps given a last chance.
When I was at home on a visit
with girls from school,
sleeping over,
we waited until mother
and my younger sisters were asleep.

***

On a school trip to Germany
in the following spring
Jeff and I took off by train
from dreary Lübeck
to the much cooler Reeperbahn
in Hamburg.

We looked for drugs in pharmacies
and checked out the latest vinyls
in small record shops.

We found a single
with a band
we had never heard of:
Jimi Hendrix Experience.
On the train home
the pills from the pharmacy in Hamburg
kicked in
and evoked nightmares.

***

Back in school
we played Purple Haze
and Hey Joe
so loud in the school's large social hall
that one of the speakers cracked.

The Christian headmaster
came running across the grass
in the darkness of the night,
ranting like a bear on speed.
Reluctantly we switched off
our new acquaintance.

The music became
more and more important
and the road away from all
that felt so meaningless.

***

One night I woke up in my bed,
everything seemed frightening.
I heard sounds outside my door.
I tried the bedside lamp,
but it didn't work.

I got out of bed,
opened the door
and peeked out into the corridor.

A chaos of hands
stretched towards me
and in panic I slammed the door shut.
I crawled back into bed.
Suddenly, everything felt better.
The lamp worked again.

**

There was a dirt road
not far from the boarding school.
One spring day I sat there
with my thumb up in the air.

I could really feel that life was there,
somewhere along that road,
somewhere, just not where I was standing.
I ended up back in Stockholm.

**

I never consciously looked for him
among the heavy shadows
of the high-rise office buildings.
In scruffy neighborhoods
he was unsought for, unanswered.

I did not knowingly
seek a fatherly figure,
but they came and went
in an endless flow
over the years
before I finally became one myself.
Not even in the destructive fires
I started in loss and confusion
could I catch a glimpse of him.

***

The adult world was rapidly
turning into something alien,
repugnant and totally unacceptable.
Broken moments
glittered alluringly on the wet asphalt.

It was 1966.
It was a new era,
a new world.
New births flowed
with new eyes
through the air that saw me.

Truths were spoken in dark clubs,
among the wildest gangs
revolt pointed a cheeky finger
to the sky.

Something rare
moved slowly
under my bare skin.
Everything was intensified
and days became springboards
to the unknown.

All around the city we
discover oases of pure beauty,
abounding with immediate experiences
and a longing for the sky.

Parks, cemeteries and rare courtyards
all were magical places
where I lit my chillum.

The sparrows spoke my language
and gulls had names of their own.
Each plant and shrub
spoke of a new, richer life.

***

The seasons followed me
and the mingling for a new, richer life,
with so many amazing promises,
became a trampoline,
but also bred an impatience
that soon, without control,
would set fire to all conventions.
Streets called on me
with their wet, shiny asphalt,
with their condemned houses
and a pungent smell of freedom.

Strangers offered me
new dreams
and a new belonging.

***

She looked like Joan Baez
and she inaugurated me
in the white stone mysteries
that both wise men and fools
call their own.
She gave me Preludin,
an amphetamine
that I swallowed at my mother's place
one day when she was not home.
Lodaren, with his oversized overcoat,
gave me a first shot in a stairwell
somewhere in the old Klara district.

The whirlwind that took me then
blew my destiny through a year
of obsessive quests
for the ultimate kick
and visits to the Epidemic Hospital
in Roslagstull.
The sky lowered itself

over the Sergel Square
and the terrace above the cinema
received pure darknes.
At times we sat
many late nights
with our pipes
and long conversations.
The journey
began without a goal.

***

My mother would often look for me
on Plattan, the paved square
next to a huge building site
outside the Central subway station.
The Stockholm cultural centre
was not yet built.
Sometimes, I followed her home.

Mom contacted a doctor
to talk about my dope smoking.
He said: Mrs. Björklund,
it is the same as if you were to drink
a glass of beer on a Friday.
That explanation my mother never could understand.

***

She was beautiful as was my longing.
I saw how she moved
across the platform
at the Hötorget subway station.
Long brown hair,
a face
reminiscent of Catherine Deneuve.

Together we moved
into an abandoned apartment
in the old and condemned Klara quarters.

46

All we needed we gathered
in the quiet and dark five story building
we had chosen,
stuff people had left behind.

We found carpets and furniture,
a mattress and some blankets.
We lived without water, without power,
in a deserted house by candlelight.
She was so beautiful.

***

But our story was short.
I met a group of young people
coming with the subway.
We started to make deals,
we all used amphetamine.

One evening
we shot Nembutal capsules
in a basement
in a southern suburb.
I fell like timber.

***

Then again I traded
the southern suburbs gang
for a cooler city gang.
Kåre, Cesar, Terje, Yngve and Olle
embraced me.

Olle would much later
travel to India
and learn to live
under the curse of the white horse.
Impressions were
pushed forward.

We ruled without weapons
and outside the law,
we made our living
as freedom fighters,
without the possibility of turning back.

I was treated with a loving respect
and cultivated a new sunshine
with breathtaking moments
of pure attention.
Money rolled in,
money rolled out.

One day short of money
we gave the dope a bath
to make it weigh more.
It was impossible to smoke
until it was dry again.

***

One day we went to Oslo
in two American cars
leased from Music Transport.
It had psychedelic posters
all over it.

We cruised around
the center of Oslo for a while,
before taking a room
in a fancy hotel.

We walked out into the city
hooking up with a bunch
of cute girls.

My girl was a blossom
and a sweet mystery in my arms.
so beautiful.

She bathed in my eyes
and my teenage lust
found an answer
to an unspoken yearning.
Young and high like I,
she was a true love of mine.

I never saw her again.

***

I remember Yngve
and his father,
both peeing in the kitchen sink,
they had no toilet.

I often visited Kåre.
One evening,
we were with the same girl.
The first Gonorrhea was a fact.
We went to the clinic
together.

***

Observation and thought
danced in gray fur
past the fragile,
with rites of their own
of all that mattered.

Moments when the inland sea
bared its confused crest
the eye of my I warmly
shook aside.
I rarely made a difference
between time and no time.

***

49

One night I was thrown out
of an apartment in Birger Jarlsgatan,
a street at the center of Stockholm.
I had been standing in the hall,
staring at the mail drop
for hours.

After what seemed an eternity
I slowly made it
all the way down the stairs.

Down by the entrance
I saw how the metal grid
around the elevator
changed color and rose
like a purple ladder
up through the old house.

On the ledge above me
two uniformed beings
called me with terrifying
curved index fingers,
half-pillars, half men.

In glass reflections
lots of people were on the move.
It was totally quiet.
It was well after midnight.

I ran up the stairs and met
the early newspaper delivery man
coming down the stone clad stairs
with chains trailing behind him.

When he threw all his newspapers
up in the air and screamed
running down the stairs
the door to the apartment opened
and I was allowed in.

***

I was seventeen, far beyond childhood
and the arms of my birth family,
unable to turn back.
I met all the cool guys
who had been around for awhile.

Travelers to and from India,
old beats still cradling
the protest like a wild garden,
created the space I needed,
but I didn't have a clue.
The world I was in was growing.

The man that was in charge
of the boys' home
at the Vitabergs Park,
where I sometimes took refuge
to have a roof over my head,
food and some warmth,
said the last time he saw me:
"If you do not change your ways,
you will become a hobo
traveling the world."
Nothing could have pleased me more.

There were several places
to to go:
the youth hostel at Slussen,
and a multitude of decent crash pads
around the city.

In the summer,
cemeteries and parks
would do,
or beautiful staircases
in old buildings.
Sometimes I was home.

***

Nights on The Barge,
a barge dockeded
at the Norr Mälarstrand pier,
were full of soul.
Otis Redding, James Brown
and The Temptations
squeezed the simmering nights
on the packed Barge
until dawn
sailed in over the water
on unruffled gull wings.

At dawn as birds ruled
the sleeping city,
a lone walker could maintain
the inner light
before the magic ended
and day regained its pulse.

The empty city woke
into a new day
with bright facades
and surfaces
Seurat would have loved.

The walker had many names.
All were not forgotten.

***

Filips, the first psychedelic club,
opened its doors
and in the light of strobes
we danced to Baby Grandmothers,
Hansson and Karlsson live.
The Doors, Jimi Hendrix, The Who
and The Mothers of Invention

put a stamp on our experience
in a true mosaic sense
from across the water.

One day my mother
found a whole new set
of glass syringes
in my pockets.

She broke down.

She often would find me
on Plattan
and would take me home
to food and a moment of warmth
before I would run off again.

***

A short time I did raw opium
instead of Preludin and Ritalina.
We cooked the opium in tablespoons,
the liquid was drawn into a syringe
through a small bit of cotton.

Sometimes we used the water
straight from Lake Mälaren.

***

A new brilliant era
with a Longing that Saved my Days
suddenly raised the streets
from their strongholds,
coloring the city
and its sky
with completely new dreams
of a world with a new meaning.
The year was 1966.
We often hung out

on any given street
watching how it undulated
like on a huge wave.
The cars went up and down
in an evocative billowing
like a slow surf.
Something woke up
and something was irrevocably gone.

***

One night I walked confused
up and down the streets of Stockholm
in bits and pieces. Too much acid.

All the bits and pieces whispered
confused directions
beneath a sky
that should have been me:
Go across the street!
Do not cross the street!
Turn right!
Turn left!

I must have looked weird.
One step straight ahead,
next to the side,
then another the other way,
all the time.

I should have been at the Concert Hall,
listening to The Mothers of Invention
that night.
I heard a totally different music,
I remember thinking.
A rough brush
is cleaning up my brain.
I tried in vain to make it
to somewhere, anywhere,
all throughout the night.

At dawn,
I met my friends.

Then we played cards
in my old bedroom
while I returned
in both voice
and undivided presence.

***

One day I walked into Åhléns,
the biggest department store
in central Stockholm,
mostly because it was warmer there.
At the subway entrance
there was a flower department.

In passing I noticed
wooden boxes
stacked with cacti.

I read the name
Lophophora Williamsii
on a small wooden stick
in one of the boxes.

A few weeks earlier I had read Huxley
and I knew exactly what this was:
A whole box
full of mescaline cactus.

I hid two cacti
beneath my Afghan sheep coat
and walked out
into the stone clad Plattan.
I sold them
for twice the price.

I bought four new cacti
that I rapidly sold
to the selling pitch of:
"Get your own peyote!"
I kept on buying and selling
until the boxes were empty.

That night me and Kåre
made a mean fruit salad
mixed with cacti
at the home of some chicks
on the island of Reimers holme.

It tasted so bitter.
And we waited.
To make sure
we took some acid too.

When we left the girls at midnight
a lit full moon shone above us,
the air was crystal clear
and it was very icy,
we were living in a cartoon.

***

Me and the The Jew were hiding
between a big pillar
and one of the large windows
in the subway station
facing Plattan
smoking a pipe.

Suddenly the window broke.
Everything happened very quickly.
I laying there on a bed of glass shards,
people standing in a circle
around me.
I thought that the window
was probably expensive,

so I got up on my feet.
Then I saw my hand
sliced by the glass
and the blood gushing.

I ran up to the roundabout
around the glass sculpture
and saw a police car.
My hand was bleeding a lot.

The police helped me into the car
and drove me
with sirens and lights flashing
to the Serafimer Hospital.

The skin on the palm of my hand
was tough and gave the needle resistance.
Seven stiches. It hurt a lot.

I also needed five stitches
on my left thigh.

***

That summer we lived
in an old wooden house
on the island of Stora Essingen,
we jammed and watered our pipes
down by the lake.

Her name was Riitta,
she was a year older than I,
but as tall as I was.
She moved in with me
for a few months.
She longed for a child
she had left back in Helsinki.
Woody also lived with us.
He came as a deserter
from the American army in Germany

and did not want
to go to Vietnam.

Big John was also a deserter
from the army
and was enchanted
with Sweden and the girls.
Big with Irish blood,
he roared against family
and subservent power.
Partying was to be his downfall.

He slept
a few cold autumn nights
on the porch.
That he told me
many times
until his time ended.
He was brutally stabbed
in his own apartment
many years later.

***

Crisp winds lifted
the eye's curtain,
the underground
becames an Olympic kaleidoscope
against time
and unforeseen possibilities.

***

The summer sun turned somersaults
over the lush lawns
of the Kungsträdgården park
and Sergeant Pepper marched
with his rainbow stretched,
arrow ready. The year
was 1967.

Jefferson Airplane constantly
took off from the bushes
and Bom Shankar
was a tribute in fashion.
The door was wide open,
the congestion
on the threshold
was palpable.

***

A sadhu I was
and the holy shaped itself
into a mythical cloud,
wandering from traveler to traveler.

Everyone who came back
from India
was dressed in thin
white cotton clothes.

So there I too walked in
the same white garment,
with my Chillums
and the embroidered bag from Nepal.

Parks and cemeteries
were sacred places
where we gathered to pay tribute
to the magnificent and unique
that was on the way.
The music
was transforming the world.

***

With the mystique
darkness grew.
Days were lost
in an ungraspable distance,

the surface appeared
increasingly
as an encoded chimera,
and the observer was fragmentized
on his way
into the chatter of details.
To leave your old life behind,
without regrets,
to delve deep
into a new state of being,
into your own true worth,
was a slow march against the wall.

***

One evening we sat
in a dark Strömparterren,
a small island
at the center of Stockholm.

We sat in an
open air café
closed for the night
and smoked our pipes.

Two police officers arrived
with Alsatians on leash.
Everyone threw their dope away,
but not me, I was too stingy,
I kept it in my pocket.

The police searched us thoroughly.
One of them found
five grams of hash in my pocket
and asked me what it was.
I have no idea, I replied, dirt?
He tossed it away
without a clue of what it was.
They were disappointed
not to have found any illegal pills.

Later that night
me and my friends were back,
looking between the tables,
but found nothing in the darkness.
A few months later
I sat on the lawn
at Klara cemetery when Klam,
a well-known social worker
and former police officer,
showed up with two police men.

I just sat there.
As if he knew where to look
he snatched up
more than one hundred grams
of Indian hash mixed with opium
out of my inside pocket.

Another night spent
at Kronoberg police station
and again, I was free in the morning.

***

During some
crazy summer days
in an old house in Lund,
a city in southern Sweden,
we spent nights on our backs
on a house roof
trying to contact aliens.
We made no contact
but had an extracorporeal experience.
The amphora was filled
until all eyes gleamed.
We could all hear and see
how the other
was closing in,
in a scary manner.

***

Back in Stockholm,
I helped a few Danes
to sell twenty kilos of Lebanese.
As a thank you,
I went with them to Copenhagen
and picked up
two hundred and fifty grams
of Lebanese hash for my trouble.
I carelessly put it
in my Nepalese shoulder bag.

It was the second time
I was outside Sweden.
I wore my Afghan coat,
Frye boots,
red corduroy pants
and I had long hair.

As I approached the ferry terminal
on my way back to Malmö
I realized I should hide the stuff.
Once aboard the boat,
I ventured into the John
and strapped the dope across my chest
with my belt.

When the boat stopped in Malmö
and I walked down the gangway
down to the dock,
I could feel how the dope
slipped out of the belt
and landed on the lining
of my trousers.

I panicked and felt my heart palpitating.
Behind a long counter leading
through the customs barracks
customs officers lined up.

The way out felt endless.
I stared straight ahead
where I could see the day light
waiting for me.
The last customs officer
beckoned to me.
He took me into a small, special room
and asked me to undress.

I peeked at him
and noticed that he was very busy
going through everything
in my magic bag.

I squeezed the big piece down
so that it slid down
the inside of a pant leg,
landing on the boot shaft
inside the pants.

I stripped my upper body
and put my clothes on a chair.
I started to take my boots off,
they had zippers.

First I unzipped one and then the other.
The dope fell on the floor
with a loud thud.
I thought, it's all over,
and turned around.
The customs man
was still rummaging through my bag.
I quickly snatched the hash
and hid it under my clothes,
lying on the chair.

I undressed until I was stark naked,
and said, with a pounding heart:
"You see, I have nothing."
Reluctantly

he let me get dressed again.
When it was time for the boots,
I turned my head and I saw
that the customs man
was once again
going through the contents
of my mystery bag,
probably desperate,
looking for something
to book me for.

I quickly grabbed the hash
from the chair
and put it into my boot,
pulled the zipper up
and put the rest of my garment
in the right place
and made it for the sunshine.

***

In Malmö I met Kenneth
listening to Bob Dylan
days on end.
I also met his sister Alice.
Together, me and Alice,
decided to make it to India.
She had some money,
I was completely broke again.
I was also awaiting trial
for multiple cannabis possessions.

She bought me a passport
from a guy who needed money.
He was shorter than I,
but like me
had mixed colored eyes.

We took the ferry to Copenhagen
and hitchhiked through Denmark.

We took the ferry from Rødby.
When we got to customs in Puttgarden
the customs officer looked
for a long time at my passport
and my heart was almost exploding.
But he let us pass.

On the highway outside the ferry terminal,
we caught a ride from a truck driver
going to Austria.

Suddenly he dropped us off
in the middle of the night.
We had no clue where we were.

Soon we had a new ride with a nice man
who said that he and his wife
ran a small hotel nearby
and that we could stay there overnight.

We woke up the following morning
to a magnificent view.
Through our window
we saw the Alps in all directions.

***

For a few days the skies
over Europe's southbound routes were open.
It was autumn,
and the journey provided a sanctuary.
I was on my way
to India.

For a while
borders were real
and the apparent rested temporarily
in its dark cocoon.

***

We hitchhiked through Yugoslavia.
At the border to Greece
we took the train
into Turkey.

When the train
rolled into Istanbul's Central station
begging children flocked around us.

We got an inexpensive Dolmuş
that took us to Sultan Ahmed
and to the Pudding Shop,
a well-known coffee shop
where a young man told us
of a cheap hotel called Gülhane.

My Universities

That autumn campfires
at the Gülhane Hotel
burned incessantly
with a chemical light.

We danced on the roof
in slow motion
with Rommelar in our blood
nights before the minaret singing
abruptly was encoded.

***

A French woman,
a few years older than I,
seduced me
and we had amazing sex.

Alice left me
and went by herself to India.
I had no money
and survived by collecting
returnable cans and bottles.
Drugs were plentiful.

***

One day I got really sick
and vomited until feces
came out of my mouth.

***

One of the nights
on the Gülhane roof,
I found myself in the eyes
of a beautiful Japanese girl.
She was short with long black hair.

It was Yoshie,
who immediately left
her German boyfriend.

We moved into a room together.
She had twenty dollars,
enough to buy thirty grams of hash.
I started walking
along dark alleys
until I found someone
that could sell me
what I wanted.

***

One night
all references were lost.
I was suddenly dissolving,
like an uncomprehending fly
on the blank wall.
A universe of emptiness
I had become.

I had mixed amphetamines,
LSD, hash and rommelar.

Different voices came to life
and called
for an impossible rebirth.

***

Darkness disappeared
and a harsh, penetrating light,
empty and painfully naked,
revealed the observer
with nothing to say
in the backseat.

I was reduced
to a mere reflection
of the many-facetted movements
that surrounded me.
I was a mechanical puppet,
an empty echo.

I followed every train,
every time I was abandoned.

That night the door
was kicked in
and together with Yoshie
I was taken away
into a night I did not understand.

Yoshie tried to flush most of the hash
down the toilet but failed.

***

I reached the surface
at the police station
where I sat on a concrete floor
of a cell that was huge,
with several tiers rising
made from wood.
On the top the wealthy Turks sat,
drinking tea and eating well.

***

My situation didn't improve
with me not agreeing to
be their scapegoat for the murder
of four policemen.
A few days earlier,
an young American man
tried to shoot himself free
at the main police station.

71

He himself was shot down
from the roof
that he had made it to.
He was called Tom Mix
in the Turkish newspapers.

"This is going to get much worse for you",
the male Turkish interpreter
said in English.
"The police chief
does not believe you.
Confess now.
make it easier on yourself."

When I maintained
that the hash
was only for my own personal use
I was pushed down on my back
and my feet were tied with rope
to a small wooden stake.

Two policemen
at each end of the stake
lifted my feet
a meter above the floor.

When the chief of police
started the beating,
I thought to myself,
that is a stupid place
to target a beating.
The skin of the soles of my feet,
I'm sure, is much too thick.

Soon the area being hit
turned into raw flesh in uproar.
I screamed and confessed
to all I thought they wanted.
I was helped
back to the big cell.

But it was not enough.
The names I'd given them
were fictitious.
The beating was once again
aimed at
my still-aching soles
and now I named
everyone I knew.

That's something
I will have to live with
for the rest of my life.

***

A young broken man
with eyes empty as mirrors,
rejected by his surroundings,
rejected by himself,
whipped and tormented,
seeking a consolation deity,
only to find a hollow echo,
more painful
than absence itself.

When the rooster crowed
for the third time
he had betrayed not only himself
but also all
who were close to him.

Now we were four
doing time
for thirty grams of hash
and days continued
to slip away.

***

Sultan Ahmed prison
met me,

a city within a city,
worn, dirty and forlorn,
with courtyards and passages
where guards with rifles
kept track
of three thousand prisoners.

Commerce and
a continuous murmur
in an incomprehensible language
met me.
From large speakers
incessant commands I did not understand
addressed the prisoners.

It was January 1969, it was winter
and a clingy chill
kept the unheated jailhouses
continuously damp.

I got a sleeping bag
from the Swedish Consulate
and a place by a stinking drain
in what had been a kitchen.

All cells were full,
stairs, corridors
and even the benches
in the kitchen were occupied.

***

Out of dirt and misery
among bugs that bit in the night,
out of murmur and confusion,
a new voice found me.

Like a blotting paper
I absorbed the contact,
my wildest ideas

were both confirmed and mutated.
All day the speakers recited names.
The city in the city
had served its purpose.

A new prison had been built
and chained two and two
we left on a sunny winter day,
riding through distant Istanbul
in regular buses.

The buses were like hermetic fish tanks
slowly moving through Istanbul
and its unreachable reality.

We were floating in a silent bus bubble
with no prospect of contact
with the elusive outside.

***

Nothing worked
in the new prison.
Dust and cries for water echoed
in the kilometer-long corridors
of this American model hell.

The seams of our clothes
were infested with colonies of lice
that migrated in the night.

Koji and Steve
kept me with words
while the Turks rolled joints
of laurel and aspirin
for lack of the real thing.

One day all foreign prisoners
were gathered in forty small cells
situated in a cell block

with four corridors on
two floors.
The cells were open during the day.

Daytime the sliding metal door
leading to the yard was open.
The Swedish consul
gave me a volleyball net.

Many years later
the Swedish government billed me
for that net.

***

Days slowly molded themselves
into a different life
with a closeness to others
in a whole new world
birthing opportunities
for knowledge
and experience spillover.

Artists, poets, musicians
and Oriental-minded thinkers
opened unimaginable doors
to new worlds.
I was reborn out of the ashes
of what I once was.

***

It was Antonio Rasile
who first whispered to me
these new visions.

Book after book
I plowed into
the newly discovered soil of I.

Cultures, religions
and world literature
slowly filled my nameless days.

On home-made stoves
of clay and wire
connected to the lamp fixture in the ceiling,
we cooked simple food.

Beans and chickpeas,
fished out of the thin soup
that turned up every day
in steel buckets,
we cooked again
with onions, garlic and tomatoes.
Every day we got a loaf of stale bread.

***

My mother kept on fighting for me
at home in Sweden.
She worked on everyone she could.
One newspaper after another
highlighted my story.

When I asked for some new books,
she managed to get
the royal Prince Bertil
to bring a package of books to me:
The Cantos of Ezra Pound
and Structural Anthropology
by Claude Lévi-Strauss,
on his trip to Turkey.

I was constantly growing.

***

After a few trials
during the winter and spring of 1969

it was time for sentencing.
My Turkish lawyer
had warned me
that I might get thirty months.

When sentencing came
unreality once again penetrated me,
crept under my skin.
I got twelve years and three months
for hash worth 20 dollars.

Koji got eight years
and Yoshie thirty months.
Steve went free.
It felt like
a heavy door
had slammed shut for good.

***

Yoshie ended up
on the women's ward.
During one
of our few meetings,
in a visiting room
with glass between us,
Yoshie told me that she was pregnant.

I felt happy
and surprised.

I proposed to her
and a few weeks later
we got married.
The Swedish consul was our witness,
the chief warden
was in charge of the ceremony.

***

One day me and Koji
were escorted from Sagmalçilar
by two soldiers
with rifles that looked like
they came from the first World War.

A taxi staggered
through the heavy traffic
of busy Istanbul's Sultan Ahmet
down to the waterfront
by the Galata Bridge
where a ferry waited.
The harbor smelled
of new-caught fried herring
raw onion and parsley.

***

Secured to each other
with a chain and a padlock,
we left Europe behind us.

Üsküdar was approaching fast
and our short frothy freedom
was soon over.

Our first steps on Asian soil
took us to a new cab
and soon
a new heavy metal door
loomed before us.

We had arrived.
This was the Toptaşi jail.

***

There was a portico
facing different court yards
with peach and almond trees.

There you could sit in the shade
with a good book.
There was a restaurant,
a hammam and a cinema
where I saw Doctor Zhivago
dubbed into Turkish.

A newly-squashed prisoner uprising
showed traces of bullet holes
in many of the walls.
We were guided around
and got the story.

***

We paid the warden
and got our own cell
in the admissions ward.

Every night we were up.
Koji played the guitar
and wrote songs.
I did glass bead jewelry
that the Swedish consulate sold,
I wrote poems and songs
and read Hermann Hesse.

***

One day Idris and Dündar turned up,
two of the most
notorious gangsters
in Turkey at that time.

The first time I saw them,
they did a royal tour of the prison.
They showed up in our ward
flanked by the warden
and a few of the guards.

They checked us out.
Dündar asked if we smoked dope.
Koji said no.
I said yes.
He brought out
a large piece of thin turkish hash,
smiled and broke off
a large chunk,
then they left.
The Warden's face was void.

Then they took charge
of the dope business
setting a new lowest price
and they ensured that the poorest
got the few jobs that were available:
in the restaurant, the cinema
and the hammam.

In some funny way
they reminded me
of the jolly men
in the Sherwood Forest.

***

One late night,
a few months later,
our Turkish neighbors
in the cell next door
turned up,
begging us desperately
to take care of
two kilos of newly-pressed hash.
The night soldiers
patrolling the balustrade
outside the big arched windows
of our cells
had seen what went on.
Koji said no.

I said yes.
We hid the thin,
cellophane-wrapped pieces
everywhere,
in the cracks in the wall,
sewn into the mattress.

At dawn, our neighbors came back.
They had found a guard
who would carry it all
to the outside.

A few hours later
all hell broke loose.
Guards and soldiers
searched thoroughly in our cells,
but did not find anything.

***

The days
slowly went to rest.

It was a magical time.
Everyone was friendly,
the food in the restaurant was good
and the hammam was an excellent place
to meet yourself
and smoke the joints
that circulated.

One day the flu arrived.
We were both almost unconscious
with a high fever
for countless days,
but soon we returned to normal.

***

The months passed easily.
One day we were told:
It is time
to move again.
This time to Paşakapi,
a few miles north of Toptaşi.

It felt a bit sad.
We had made
so many good Turkish friends
and established a life
that was more than bearable.
Still in Sağmalçilar
were Yoshie and the others.

***

On our first day in Pasakapi
we were lodged in a cell
situated in a high wall
with a small window
with bars
facing the street.

Summer had not yet arrived.
It was chilly and damp
and we caught colds constantly.
There was no source of heat.

The entire prison was like
a Gothic nightmare
sunken down
by its own weight,
flanked by drab apartment buildings
on all sides.

The feeling of the place was heavy,
the weight of the building
made you feel like
something was sinking.

***

On our second day
Koji and I stood talking
in one of the many courtyards
when suddenly
everyone just vanished.
Even the guards were gone.

We remained where we were,
not knowing
what to expect or wait for,
not knowing what to do.

Suddenly there was a scream.
Two men entered the courtyard
running through a portal.
One was chasing the other
with a large knife in his hand.
They disappeared
up some stairs
and it was quiet again.

After a while,
guards and prisoners returned.

It had been a showdown
between two rival gangs
to determine who
should be in charge
of the hash sales,
we were later told.

***

The heavy sentences we had
crept slowly within us
in a dark momentum,
but we kept

mostly to ourselves.
We were awake all night,
slept as much as we could
during the day.

We were friends now,
but it had taken several months
before Koji spoke to me.
After all, it was my fault
that he was in prison.

***

A new summer rolled around
and it was time
to move again.

Now Koji and I
had to go back to Sağmalçilar,
back to our friends
and my heavily pregnant
Japanese wife.

***

The same day I turned twenty
the Woodstock festival started.
My mother came to visit me
along with my sister Berit.
Sussi did not want to.

In early December
the Altamont festival
set a full stop to a generation
and a decade.

***

Sağmalçilar was like coming home.
The old gang was still there

and belonging hung
like an old promise
in the hot summer air.

A new traveler
had arrived,
Chris Cheal from London.

He had toured in Sweden
with a R & B band
called Evil Eyes.
Another poet
with a wonderful voice
and a blast
playing the harmonica.

***

We were a family,
a collective
of creative men.

Antonio from Fano,
artist and poet,
India bum and biennale king,
Beat and Freak,
the man who gave my days
a new direction
and a new vast content.

Ronald, long and colored
from Chicago,
Black Panther and rabid poet,
read his poetic manifesto aloud
of black man's strength and beauty,
of white man's
decadent and moribund society.

George from Zurich
came recently

from an ashram in India
where he had studied
the Vedas and Russian mystics.

And Koji Morrishita,
the man with an eye for
the here of now
and the thoughts behind it,
the artist that finally gave me
the hills and the branches,
full of fruit,
with their impossible weightlessness.

**

I read and followed
The Living Theater of Antonin Artaud,
a fate of strong determination
bordering on the unlikely.
I traveled with him
among mescal Indians
and kept him company
during the years he spent
in mental hospitals.

**

I had long conversations
with Rabindranath Tagore
and I often woke up in Russia
in the late nineteenth century.

The Japanese slowly moved
deep into my eyes
and tales were mixed
with reality
and Dylan Thomas.

I moved through the days
like a monk in his prayers,

far away
from the surrounding turmoil
we faced every day.
The tick tock of the seasons
was so quiet.

***

During a few years
I changed my handwriting.
First, I wrote
with capital letters for a year,
then I invented a new
elaborate, cursive handwriting.

***

One night a dark presence
was born in my dream mouth.
It was hairy with many legs.

That darkness scared me
and it grew until I decided
that something had to be done.
I bit with everything I had.
The relief and joy in that moment
was indescribable.
I felt proud when I woke up.

***

My teeth were in a bad state
and I suffered
more and more toothaches.

A dentist received me
in a small cell,
connecting the drill
to the lamp socket in the ceiling.
A small electric motor hung

in a leather strap around his neck
he dragged the drill
behind him
on the floor
when he walked.

He drilled for a while,
put some cotton into the cavity
and covered it with wax.
When my toothache
eventually became unbearable
he pulled the aching tooth out.
The apertures were growing.

***

We hung our unbleached cotton sheets
in front of the bars
to increase
our personal, life-loving
proximity to light,
wind and space.

Playfully the wind
grabbed the fabric
speaking of a world that waited for us.

Secrets grew
like glowing spheres
in our gatherings and meetings
with the amazing.

Sufi men we were
and Zen spelled summer.
When we showered in cold water,
Ganesh laughed.

***

I learned to do the sun salutation
and there was a story
going around
of an imprisoned tiger
in a small cage,
continuously activating
all his muscles in this manner.
I learned to meditate,
sitting still without thoughts,
without not thinking,
leaving the observer
and the one observing
the observer that observed.

I have never been so tanned
like I was that summer,
but the summer eventually grew cool
and autumn came with melancholy
and a longing for completeness.

Myths born in solitude
danced with ritual twists
and I followed them
to the door.

***

In September, Christina had been born.
She spent her first year
with Turkish prisoners
in the women's ward.

It was a strange feeling
to suddenly have a family,
to be a father for a family
that I only could see
with my inner eye.
I had a baby girl
that I only saw a few times,

but I was a very proud father,
dreaming of a future.

***

In the dark of the Turkish night
I found a faithful friend
who followed me
all through the years
- Orion.

Wherever I was, I saw him
and found my position.
When winter came,
he glittered at his most at dawn.

The radio played organ fugues
of Johan Sebastian Bach
at the break of dawn.
Three cats
were sleeping at my feet.

***

I had come far.
I was on a mission.
This was my life.

***

That winter sucked all life
out of our ice-blue days
with their elevated skies.

The dove on the wall
talked of a distant freedom,
an impossible vision.

Herbs withered and died,
one by one.

The sky was graying,
the walks were increasingly
more crystallized.
We ran our thesis
against the logic of winter.
When Christmas rolled around,
we cooked something special
and spoke about
the world outside.

***

We spent those days
in constant learning
and I made so many friends,
now long dead.

I slept on a blanket
that I had spread
over the wooden boards of the bed.
Stretched out and collected
I met the night.

Pigeons received me at dawn
and gave to me a winged temple
where I could meet the day.

When the first snow fell,
birthing my northern memories
with chilly winds,
I often whispered your name.

Visions of childhood
crept like pale phantoms
through my world.

***

When almost two years had gone by,
there was no other alternative.
I lived here and now.

Each day's reality
transcended its momentary content
and life outside
slowly faded in importance.

Through a small window
at the back in the wall
I could see Turkish children playing
on the dusty street outside.
I could see the water man
coming down the road
with a donkey before his cart,
loaded with fresh water.

***

I often saw the hare
jumping in the full moon
in a Japanese way.
At times I thought of the darkness
that gave birth
to the spider in my mouth.

One time I dreamed I was a deer,
performing ritual leaps
in a forest filled with myths.
Another time I saw a huge aircraft
with huge Union Jacks
fluttering from its wings
crashing into the sea
surrounding the islands of Stockholm.

***

That spring evoked other springs,
despite the scanty greenery,
struggling in the cement cracks.

I saw swallows
and I knew summer was coming.
Different myths kept me company
when I tried to learn Sanskrit.

***

First came Chris A,
arrested in a park in Istanbul
with a few grams of dope.

Then his stepson Timothy,
fourteen years old,
tried to sell the rest,
about ten kilos,
to a man from the CIA.

They had come
all the way from India,
Chris, his wife, all the kids,
the dogs and the monkey.

The money ran out
and here they were.

Chris was a musician.
With his guitar we had a band
playing in the evening shadow.

***

This one morning,
the wind blew in a different way
and the feeling of full presence
followed the capsule

with synthetic mescaline
I had just swallowed.

It came in a package of guitar strings
from Paul who had recently left Sağmalçilar.
The huge building rolled like a ship
in the hot wind,
the cotton sheets in the windows
swirled pleasantly and promising
like sails.
The sun emptied
its exuberant color particles
and the experience
tasted of Central American cactus
and Lazarus.

We sat in a circle
on blankets
out on the yard.
When the melon was cut in half
the sky sighed and fell apart.

**

One morning I sat on my bed.
Ginger – one of our cats –
was also there, sleeping.

The cat was the first to sense
that something serious
was about to happen.

It started as a vibration.
At first, I thought it was me.

When the lamp in the ceiling
started to swing
ever more intensively and wilder
and when the bed started to move,
I too realized: Earthquake!

Everyone rushed out
into the courtyard,
hoping the wall would fall.

After a few minutes
everything was as before.
We soon got new light bulbs.

***

After twenty months,
Yoshie and Christina had been released.
Every day she wrote to me
from various places in Europe.
She folded her envelopes
from glossy magazines.

Finally, she ended up in Sweden,
where apparently
– I've been told –
it did not go too well.

***

That Christmas,
we made a candlelit mobile
of cardboard
and colored cellophane.
Two cylinders spun
in opposite directions
with fans driven by the heat
from home-made oil lamps.

Stars and planets, mythical creatures,
flowers and birds,
everything danced back and forth
on the large grease-paper screen
placed in front of the cylinders.
The cylinder's cut-outs

met and separated,
constantly shifting colors.

Even the prison director
spent some time with us that night,
fascinated by the show.

***

When I first heard the word,
I thought of Camus.
However, the rats,
large like beavers,
still made it up
through the hole in the toilet floor
between the footsteps.

We read
in the Turkish papers
how the plague raged
outside the walls,
the hospitals were overcrowded,
many died.

We were all vaccinated
with one giant syringe
with enough vaccine
for a whole ward.

No one had ever heard of
blood contamination.

In our besieged city
the wait during the cholera epidemic
was long indeed.
Visits were forbidden
and I thought of Camus.

***

Billy showed up one day,
a young and positive
American with juggling balls
and a neon-colored frisbee.
He was happy until the day
he got sentenced.
It got worse
when the prosecutor succeeded
in his appeal.
Billy got thirty years
for his two kilos.
We spent many hours together
talking about everything
and nothing.

He eventually gravitated
towards the heavier birds,
those who always crowed
with dissatisfaction
with no possibility
of seeing the whole picture.

He wanted to escape. And he did.

***

One day there was a commotion
between German Hans and Ziat,
the Syrian guy in charge of tea
and dope.

After a dispute
Ziat threw Hans' cat
down the garbage chute,
never to be seen again.

***

Hans boiled cough medicine
that he injected.

Then there was Heinz, a magpie man,
short and strong.
Claudio was the expert
on what was of value
in the old Byzantine churches
dotting the Turkish country side.
and took it with him.

A society within a society,
forced into a new seeing
with pale presence moving along
in days that rarely
were enough.

***

Every year my mother came
for my birthday in August.
This year she brought Gösta,
her new partner,
a man I immediately grew to like.
He was academically educated,
his father had been the head of
United Artists in Sweden,
but he himself had gone bankrupt
and drove a taxi.

It was the start of a friendship
that ended many years later
when he died of cancer.

***

Koji woke me up one morning.
He was back from the jail
on the Imrali island
where he had been sent a few months earlier.

I fixed breakfast
with goat cheese, black olives,

eggs, oranges, yogurt
and the day-old Turkish bread.

Chris told me later that day
that the Vietnam war was over.
Was it really true?
I sure hoped so.

That day was canteen day
and everybody restocked
with groceries for sale.
Each day the sun
crept further and further
down into the courtyard.

Soon we could walk
on the concrete
with the sun in our faces.

***

On consulate day
in the morning,
staff from the Swedish, American,
Austrian, Swiss, French
and British consulates
arrived.

Swift motions, movements
and a lot of small talk.

One by one
we came back
from our visitor's time
with plastic bags
filled with cookies and chocolate.

Chris had gotten permission
to let his hair grow long.
It was officially forbidden,

but the biggest zealot
concerning shaving and haircut
was Necdet, our Syrian fellow prisoner,
presently running our place.

Necdet was a condemned spy
and a colder person
I have never met.
Since a few months back
I had been given permission
to grow a beard.
When it got dark
it was time to prepare the food.
This day it was cooked wheat with onions.

Koji sat next to me
painting.
No consular visits for him today.
The Japanese consul
only came twice a year.

***

Barber day was
the only day in the week
there were Turks in in our ward.
I did prefer them
to the complex-filled Arabs
we lived with every day.

I found the time one day
to write a poem:
"Here's where one noise
replaces the next,
where the voices of tea mongers
are drowned out
by the guy that suddenly
has a visit,
where one nonsense conversation
is followed by another,

where five different radio stations
are on the air
at the same time,
where the grating sound of
heat fans never cease.
It is not always easy
to do something creative here.
I miss the one man cells
we had before.
But they were given
to the anarchists of Istanbul."

***

I got up early in the morning.
Before it got cold
I used to get up at 4 am,
do my yoga
and have two hours
before anyone woke up.

Doves were flying around
in the courtyard.
Someone had strewn breadcrumbs
for them.

Around 8 am
all my fellow prisoners
had woken up.

In this place
you could get out of bed
whenever it pleased you.
There were no guards there
except for at sayem,
when we all stood in line
to be counted each night.
It took about two minutes.

The next two days
were floor-scrubbing days,
pushing water across the floor
with reed brooms
from one end to the other.

The medanci was back
with a cloth sack
filled with the day's bread.

A medanci was someone
who for a small sum
did all the odd work.
It was a hard job.

***

The sun was warm.
There was a vague hint
of a new spring to come,
hanging elegantly in the air.

Despite all the heaviness
that rolled around in our days
there was a lot of light
shining through,
so many vast experiences,
so many amazing people.

Everything
that was experienced
as dark and foreboding,
seemed like nothing when
it was over.

Four years had gone
since Koji and I were relocated
from the old Sultan Ahmed jail
to this new Sağmalçilar jail.
What a motley crew we were.

Chained two and two
we had moved in buses
to this place.
3000 prisoners.

We were first put together
with Turkish hash smokers
according to the order
of crimes committed.

There were many Turks
doing time there for a drug
that was cultivated all over the place
and used by so many.

***

I woke up early
this morning as well.
It was January 29, 1973.

I did my exercises
and finished with a cold shower.

The weather had softened,
the indoor temperature
was rather bearable now.

A young French guy
made bail today
and after a few dealings
Koji got the bunk above mine.

Went to the photographer today
to take photos for some formality
or other.
The photographer insisted
that he knew me
from the time I was free

in his Istanbul
more than four years ago.

Walking back through
the long corridors
I met Hamido, the chief of guards,
I had seen him
and his second-in-command Arif Topuz
brutally beat prisoners,
and some of us.
They were the dread and fear
of this jail world.

I wondered if the prison director
really knew what went on
when he was not around.

The Return

The message came in the morning:
Pack your things.
You're going home in the afternoon.

Spring was in the air
and it had been well over four years
since the police
kicked in the door of my hotel room.

I packed and said goodbye
to all too many years,
from friends and suspended time,
with mixed feelings,
with a new vision in my eyes.

Just the thought
of flying gave me a high.
But I was briskly
brought back to earth
hard and ruthlessly.

I was brought to the Istanbul airport
in handcuffs.
There a Swedish policeman
from Interpol awaited.

Following a ritual change
of national handcuffs,
I went with my new companion
onto the plane.

I was a routine job, an easy way
to make some extra money.
He didn't even talk to me,
this hardened criminal
he had to pick up.

At Arlanda airport,
my mother, Gösta and my sisters
were waiting with flowers

and longing.
But I was led out the back door
to a prison transport.

Only after insistent inquiry
did my family find me,
locked up in the back seat
of a black, fortified sedan.

I received long hugs
through the car window
before I was driven
to the Österåker
maximum security jail.

**

I ended up in the intake
as if I had just been busted,
some uninteresting wreckage
that just washed up,
a criminal
among all the others.

I was stripped of all my belongings,
clothes, books and instruments.

After a month of isolation
there was an important meeting.
I was offered a job
at the toy workshop.

When I refused
on grounds
that I should not even be there
and said I wanted to be an artist,
I was offered isolation
with an opportunity to paint.
It was my twelve-year sentence
that hung in the balance,

twelve years for twenty bucks
worth of turkish hash.

**

I waited eagerly for my colors,
panels, palete and brushes.
After two weeks in wait
in solitary, the chief warden
finally returned from his leave:
"I know the likes of you.
You paint on the walls
and in general, destroy.
You can forget about painting.
I'm the one in charge here."

A week later,
the management made a round.
I described what had happened,
and after indignant dismay
paints and other things
promptly appeared.
Finally I painted with oil colors
for the first time in my life.

**

One day there was a letter from Yoshie
saying that she wanted a divorce.

I refused.
Then there was a letter
from her boyfriend,
the same German
she had been with
when we met on the roof
of the Gülhane.

He wrote that it didn't matter
if I signed or not,
she belonged to him.

Under protest,
I wrote my signature
upside down.

***

A few months later
a new letter
was given to me.
Yoshie wanted to give up Christina
and there wasn't much
I could say or do
due to my predicament.

I was so saddened by the loss
of both Yoshie
and Christina.
I had been waiting for so long.

***

It was obvious
that the prison bureaucrats
were fooling me:
I had to work in solitary,
folding plastic collection-bags
and putting them in large paper envelopes;
or glue Nordic flags
on thin strings,
ready for the Christmas tree.

I came up with an idea.
I asked the man in the next cell
and he gladly made a double quota
for straight cash.
So I bought and sold

and painted full time
in my new hermitage.
In this jail I didn't wear
my own clothes,
I had no responsibility
of my own
for what the day might hold,
nor did I have a defense
against the cold,
insect-like
observation.

This was heavy punishment indeed
for something that in Sweden
would render a fine.

***

Out on the exercise yard,
the slice you get
from the full circle,
with a guard tower
at the center,
poems were born
in the meeting
with the northern pine forest.

The extinguished eye
of Polyphemus
rested above me.

When the scent of autumn
matured with promises
of fruit and freedom
I was offered something new:
Go to the open Svartsjölandet jail.
You don't have to work there either.

***

In the fall of 1973
I stood in an apple orchard.
Images of imagination
and reality
slowly gained access
to who I was.

The wall was replaced
with a picket fence,
a path led straight out
into a new eternity.

I walked out into the fall
on a dirt road at dusk
under a sky
no less than immense.

Heavenly harbingers
of storm and darkness
lifted me ever higher
as I moved
further away from
everything that had been.

All that was wild and untamed
grew with what
forest, animal
and open distance could offer.

The world vibrated
in the smallest atom
and everything was just as important,
except that which was obscured.

An abandoned house
at the edge of the road
offered a ghostly shadow play.
Trees spoke to me
of the speed of perception
and of everything

that lay within the possibilities
of angular occurrence.

There in the dark
I was reborn
with full strength.
The hegemony of low colors
faded in that presence.
I was home.

***

Two weeks later,
the King's pardon fell
like a ripe autumn apple
into my hand,
in this strange garden
where Eve for such a long time
has been an impossible dream.

***

The first few days of freedom
were shy and see-through.
Everyone looked at me
with strange looks.
Traveling on the subway
turned into torment.

I walked a lot on
the streets of Söder,
the southern part
of downtown Stockholm,
this damp autumn,
writing countless poems
in my notebook.

I received a bill
from the Ministry of Foreign Affairs
for every single dollar

they had spent on me
during my time in Turkey,
six dollars a week
plus, the volleyball net ...

New Goals

I lived for a few weeks
in Gösta's apartment
on the Vulcanusgatan Street,
by the railroad tracks
down in the Atlas area,
central Stockholm.

We often
sat up late at night.
We both painted
and I wrote.

In the window
the mobile
I received from Koji
hung.

New passport
and off again.

$$***$$

Postlude

The young man I was
travelled far
and lived in many countries.

I finally returned
to my native Sweden
in the spring of 1990.

I started to study English
at Stockholm University,
even though I never went
to high school.

I got a job at an old people's home
and tried to forget
the jealous Wilzamara Santos Machado
I left behind in a favela
in Rio de Janeiro

***

In 1996 I met Harvey Cropper,
an American artist and a good friend
of Charlie Parker.

Harvey saw the artist in me
and I spent years
at his top floor studio,
starting a brand-new set
of intensely coloured canvases.

One month after meeting Harvey
I met my present wife Gertrude
while rehearsing
with my old friend Kåre
and some other musicians.

She was sitting in the kitchen
and I remember thinking:
There she is!

We got married in an old
wooden church
on a hill overlooking
the south of Stockholm.

I got a job as a journalist
and we had two beautiful children,
a girl and a boy,
who became our gifts to the future.

***

I started to work for a Roma magazine
with news pertaining
to the Roma people in Sweden
and the rest of the world.

***

"Hurry up Fred
we're gonna miss
the damn airplane!"

After three days in Pristina
taking notes
at a Roma summit
we were heading home.

Civil Rights Defenders
had once again
invited the unwanted.

***

Tuva my youngest daughter
has finished high school
and works at a preschool.

My son Lucas
dreams of a future
far from mine. Works in a supermarket.

There is love in that too.

***

It seems not so long ago now
that my hot Brazilian years
rattled my existence
into survival and romance.

The umbilical cord
of new-born Joía
was buried by the waterfall
next to a ritual glass of caçasa
and a cigar gone out.

Me and my American wife Rose
toured for a year with Beto Quadros
in the state of São Paolo
before I turned baker in Rio.

The last three years in Brazil
I ran my own employment agency
in the favela Vila Parque da Cidade.

The wild Mara
once busted my foot
after three days of fighting.

That night I jumped on one leg
down the steep alleys,
caught a ride with the school bus,
that made a detour to the hospital.

My friendship with Ronald Biggs
made the chief of the favela
open his door

and his little bags
of green and white fun.
Going with the old tram
up to favela of Santa Teresa
put me right back into the movie
Orpheu Negro.

***

I took some computer classes
At the Royal Technical college
and modern philosophy
at the Uppsala university.

Harvey Cropper was family,
integrity and a well of knowledge
inspiring me on my way.

***

After 18 years
my work as a journalist
at the É Romani Glinda magazine
suddenly ended.

***

In 2015 i Performed in Wales
and did the last editing
of my first poetry collection in English.

In 2016 i was invited
to a big poetry festival
in Tanta, Egypt.

In 2017 i performed at a Roma
poetry festival in Romania.
In 2018 I was awarded

Sweden Beat Poet Laurreate
for life
by the National Beat Poetry Foundation,
based in Connecticut.

In 2019
I performed in Argentina.
Poets embraced me
when I performed.

Then there was
Corona.

***

Even in Sweden
I am finally recognized as a poet,
an artist and a muscian.
It only took 50 years

***

The psychotic young man
I once was
entered a life of constant learning
in the jails of Istanbul.

A lifelong journey,
a fearless journey,
riding wild storms,
holding onto visions
of human magnitude.

I will not yield
to the common sleep
of men in anger,
nor die for a cause
that is all about
indecency.

Other published works by Bengt O Björklund

Det genombrutna fönstret, Inferi, 1975 (poetry)
Nådsökarna, Inferi, 1978 (poetry)
Att älska, CD, Varg publishing, 2002 (poetry recited to music)
Staden, interactive, a long poem on CD-rom, Utposter, 2004
Jag missade Woodstock, Podium, 2009 (this book in Swedish)
Funderingar, with Angelica Wiik, Podium, (Poetry with art by
Angelica Wiik)
Vi drömde om en cirkus, Fel förlag, 2013, (autobiografi in verse)
Bakro, comic series with Ulf Lundkvist, ERG förlag, 2015
Singing in my Chains Like the Sea, Iconau, 2015 (poetry)
I, Middle Creek Publishing, 20018 (poetry)
A stab in the dark, alien Buddha Press, 2018 (poetry)
Humility is not the name of a strange bird, National Beat Poetry
Foundation Inc, (poetry) 2019
I missed Woodstock, Human Error Publishing, 2020
All––a dessa årstider Haiku, Fri Press, 2023

124

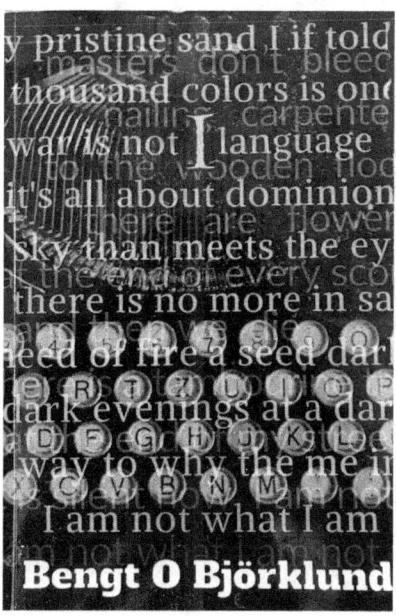

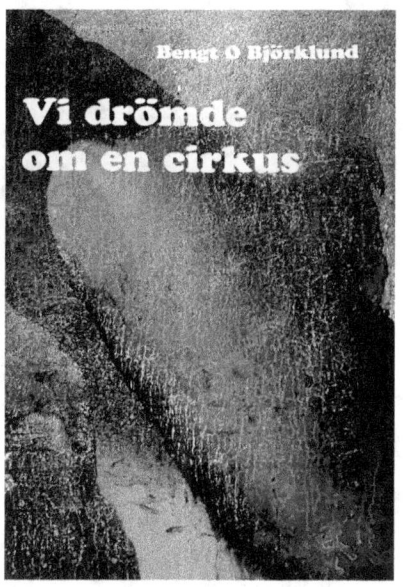

1964   1968   1969   1971

Sweden Beat Poet Laureate - lifetime